Karen'

Other books by
Ann M. Martin

P. S. Longer Letter Later
(written with Paula Danziger)
Leo the Magnificat
Rachel Parker, Kindergarten Show-off
Eleven Kids, One Summer
Ma and Pa Dracula
Yours Turly, Shirley
Ten Kids, No Pets
With You and Without You
Me and Katie (the Pest)
Stage Fright
Inside Out
Bummer Summer

For older readers:

Missing Since Monday
Just a Summer Romance
Slam Book

THE BABY-SITTERS CLUB series
THE BABY-SITTERS CLUB mysteries
THE KIDS IN MS. COLMAN'S CLASS series
BABY-SITTERS LITTLE SISTER series
(see inside book covers for a complete listing)

Little Sister

Karen's Christmas Carol

Ann M. Martin

Illustrations by Susan Crocca Tang

A
LITTLE APPLE
PAPERBACK

SCHOLASTIC INC.
New York Toronto London Auckland Sydney
Mexico City New Delhi Hong Kong

ISBN 0-590-50056-2

12 11 10 9 8 7 6 5 4 3 2 1   8 9/9 0 1 2 3/0

Printed in the U.S.A.   40
First Scholastic printing, December 1998

The author gratefully acknowledges
Stephanie Calmenson
for her help
with this book.

Karen's Christmas Carol

Together Again

"One flake, two flakes, three flakes, four! Five flakes, six flakes, seven flakes, more!"

Maybe you think I was counting cereal flakes. I was not. It was a December morning and I was counting snowflakes. They were falling outside my little house. (I have two houses — a big house and a little house. I will tell you more about them later.)

The snow was white and sparkly. It fell quietly. But it was too quiet for me. I wished someone would wake up and keep me company. But it was early Sunday morning.

Mommy, Seth (my stepfather), and Andrew (my little brother, who is four going on five) were still sleeping.

But I was wide awake. I am Karen Brewer. I am seven years old. I have blonde hair, blue eyes, and some freckles. I wear glasses. I have a blue pair for reading and a pink pair for the rest of the time. Except when I am sleeping.

Why was everyone at the little house sleeping so late? At the big house, someone is usually awake when I get up. That is because so many people live there.

I missed the big house. I had lived there since last spring. There was almost always something going on. Even early in the morning.

I closed my eyes and wished that Andrew would wake up and come downstairs. I wished very hard.

Guess what! When I opened my eyes, Andrew was standing in front of me. I jumped when I saw him. He had tiptoed into the room so quietly, I had not heard him.

"I did not want to wake you up," said Andrew.

"I was not sleeping," I replied. "I was wishing you would wake up and come downstairs."

"And I did!" said Andrew. "I am glad you are here. I woke up sad."

"What is wrong?" I put my arm around my little brother.

"I miss Chicago," Andrew replied.

Andrew lived in Chicago with Mommy and Seth for almost eight months. Seth had to move there for a very good job. (He is a carpenter.)

"I am sorry you miss Chicago. I think I know how you feel. I miss the big house," I said.

"What do you miss the most?" asked Andrew.

I had to think for a minute.

"I miss all the people and all the pets," I replied. "But especially Pumpkin, because she is such a funny kitten. And Boo-Boo, because I will never see him again."

Pumpkin was our newest pet. Boo-Boo was Daddy's cat, who died. I did not always like him so much. But Boo-Boo and I became good friends while I was living at the big house.

"What do you miss about Chicago?" I asked.

"I miss my friends at school. And my room," said Andrew.

We sat together and watched the snow come down.

"One thing I do not miss is missing you," I said.

"What?" said Andrew.

"I missed you when you were in Chicago."

"I missed you too," said Andrew.

"It is good we are here together," I said.

"Yup. You know what? I am hungry."

"Me too," I replied. "We are not allowed to cook without Mommy and Seth. But we are allowed to have cereal. Want some?"

"Yup!" said Andrew.

We raced to the kitchen. Soon my little brother and I were eating — and counting — Krispy Krunchy flakes.

I was *so* glad that Andrew was home again.

2

Happy Where I Am

It is easy to miss one place when you are someplace else. Now that I am at the little house, I miss the big house. But when I am at the big house, sometimes I miss the little house.

But wait. I was going to tell you why I have two houses. Here is the story.

A long time ago, when I was little, I lived in one house. That was the big house, here in Stoneybrook, Connecticut. I lived there with Mommy, Daddy, and Andrew.

Then Mommy and Daddy started arguing

a lot. They tried hard to work things out. But they just could not do it. So they got a divorce.

Mommy and Daddy told Andrew and me that they were divorcing each other, not us. They told us they loved each of us very much and always will. It is true.

After the divorce, Mommy moved with Andrew and me to the little house, not too far away. Then she met Seth. She and Seth got married, which is how Seth became my stepfather. So in my little-house family are Mommy, Seth, Andrew, me, Rocky (Seth's cat), Midgie (Seth's dog), Emily Junior (my pet rat), and Bob (Andrew's hermit crab).

Daddy stayed in the big house after the divorce. (It is the house he grew up in.) He met a nice woman named Elizabeth and they got married. Elizabeth was married once before. She has four children, who are now my stepsister and stepbrothers. They are David Michael, who is seven, like me; Kristy, who is thirteen and the best stepsister ever; and Sam and Charlie, who are old enough to be in high school.

My other sister is Emily Michelle. She is two and a half. Daddy and Elizabeth adopted Emily from a faraway country called Vietnam. (I love her a lot. That is why I named my rat after her.)

Another person I love a lot is Nannie. Nannie is Elizabeth's mother, which makes her my stepgrandmother. She came to live at the big house to help take care of Emily. But really she takes care of everyone. She also has a candy-making business. She makes her candy right in the big house. Sometimes I get to help and taste. Yum!

The pets at the big house are Shannon, David Michael's big Bernese mountain dog puppy; Scout, our training-to-be-a-guide-dog puppy; Pumpkin, the new kitten; Crystal Light the Second, my goldfish; and Goldfishie, Andrew's gorilla. (Just kidding!)

Before Andrew moved to Chicago, we switched houses almost every month. (I moved to Chicago too, but did not stay.)

Now that Andrew is back, we will switch houses again — one month at the big house, one month at the little house.

I gave Andrew and me special names because we have two of so many things. I call us Andrew Two-Two and Karen Two-Two. (I thought up those names after my teacher, Ms. Colman, read a book to our class. It was called *Jacob Two-Two Meets the Hooded Fang*.)

Andrew and I have two families with two mommies and two daddies. We have two sets of toys and clothes and books. And we each have two bicycles. (I am the one who taught Andrew how to ride a two-wheeler!)

I also have two best friends, Hannie Papadakis and Nancy Dawes. (We call ourselves the Three Musketeers.) Hannie lives across the street and one house over from the big house. Nancy lives next door to the little house.

So no matter which house I am living in, I have all that I need. (Unless I leave something special behind.) I can be happy where I am. Happy is a good thing to be!

10

3

Mommy's News

Mommy and Seth finally came downstairs.

"Good morning!" I said. "Would you like us to make you breakfast? How about some Krispy Krunchies?"

I picked up the box and shook it. Oops. It was almost empty. That is because Andrew and I had each eaten three bowls of cereal.

"That is all right," said Seth. "We will have toast and jam."

"Will you keep us company?" asked

Mommy. "There is something I would like to talk to you about."

"Is it something good?" I asked.

"It is something good for Mommy," Seth replied.

Seth made coffee. Mommy made toast. Then we all sat down to talk.

"A very good job has come up and I have decided to take it," said Mommy.

Andrew's eyes grew wide with worry.

"Are we moving again?" he asked.

"No, we are not moving," said Mommy. "The job is right here in Stoneybrook."

I breathed a sigh of relief.

"You know that while I was in Chicago, I learned to make jewelry. Now I have been offered a job making jewelry at the Stoneybrook Crafts Center."

Hmm. I felt confused. I knew I was supposed to be happy for Mommy. But I was scared. I guess Andrew was too. He asked the question I was thinking of myself.

"Who will take care of us?" said Andrew.

"You do not have to worry," said

Mommy. "I will not start working until I find someone very nice to be with you when I am at work."

"I do not want someone nice. I want *you*!" said Andrew. He started to cry.

"You do not have to be afraid," said Seth. "By the time the job starts, you will know your nanny very well."

"That is right. We will not leave you with a stranger," said Mommy.

Boo. I had just gotten over missing Mommy and now she was talking about leaving again. She was not going very far. She was only going to be downtown. Still, things would not be the same.

We talked some more. Andrew wanted to know why Mommy needed to take a job.

"You have a job," he said. "You are Mommy."

"Of course. And that will always be my favorite job of all," Mommy replied. "But now that you are going to school, you need me less. And we could use the extra money."

14

"Speaking of making money, I have to get to my shop," said Seth. "I have a rush order waiting. I promised to work on the weekend to have it ready tomorrow."

Our talk was over. Seth left for work. Mommy and I cleaned up the kitchen. And Andrew disappeared into the den.

4

Big Sister

After I finished helping in the kitchen, I went to the den. Poor Andrew. He was sitting in front of the TV watching a Road Runner cartoon. But he was not laughing. He looked unhappy.

It was time for action. The situation called for help from his big sister, Karen Brewer.

"What are you watching?" I asked.

"TV," said Andrew.

"I can see that. What is Road Runner up to?"

"Don't know," Andrew replied without taking his eyes off the screen.

"Well, if you are not really watching, do you want to play a game with me?"

Andrew shrugged.

"Come on," I said. "We can play something fun."

"No." Andrew made a grumpy face.

This was not working. I needed a plan. I thought and thought. Then I got an idea. I found a calendar in the kitchen. Then I ran back to the den. I stood between Andrew and the TV.

"One, two, three," I said. "Three weeks till Christmas!"

That got Andrew's attention.

"We have to start getting ready."

"What will we do?" asked Andrew.

"Lots of things. Come on, we will make a list."

I found a pencil and some paper in a drawer.

"First we will decorate the house," I said.

I wrote *Decorate house* at the top of the paper. (It is a good thing I am an excellent speller.)

"What else?" asked Andrew.

"We need Christmas cards."

"Then we will need stamps," said Andrew. "I know all about mailing letters. A letter carrier came and talked to my class at school!"

I added *Stamps* to our list.

"We need presents!" said Andrew.

"We sure do!" I wrote *PRESENTS* in capital letters.

"And we will have to wrap the presents. So we will need wrapping paper. Maybe we can make some," I said.

Andrew was starting to perk up.

Ring! Ring!

Mommy answered the phone.

"Karen, it is for you. It is Nancy," she said.

I picked up the phone.

"Hi, Nancy!" I said.

Nancy invited me to come to her house. She said Hannie would be there too.

I looked at Andrew. If I left him alone, he might get sad again. I knew what I had to do.

I do not usually invite my little brother to play with my friends and me. But this was a special occasion.

"Can Andrew come too?" I asked.

Nancy said yes. She did not seem to mind one bit.

"Come on, we have to get dressed," I said when I hung up the phone. (Andrew and I were still in our pajamas.) "We are going to play with Hannie and Nancy today. Maybe we still start making wrapping paper later."

Andrew jumped up and raced to his room. He was smiling. I was being a good big sister.

While I got dressed I thought about Christmas presents. I wanted to get a really special one for Andrew. I had three whole weeks to decide what it should be.

5

Something Exciting

On Monday something exciting happened at school. My teacher, Ms. Colman, said she had an Important Announcement to make. Ms. Colman is my favorite teacher, and Important Announcements are my favorite kind!

I turned to Hannie and Nancy and gave them the thumbs-up sign. Hannie and Nancy sit at the back of the room. I used to sit in the back with them, until I got my glasses. Then Ms. Colman moved me to the front so I could see better. (By the way, Ms. Colman is a glasses-wearer too.)

Now I sit between two other glasses-wearers. They are Ricky Torres, who is my pretend husband (we got married on the playground at recess one day), and Natalie Springer, who is always bending down to pull up her socks, which are very droopy.

I sat up tall to listen to Ms. Colman's announcement.

"I just found out that the Stoneybrook Community Center is putting on a play called *A Christmas Carol*, by Charles Dickens," said Ms. Colman. "They have found all the grown-ups for the play, and now they are looking for some children. If you would like to try out for a part in the play, please raise your hand."

My hand shot up first. I looked around the room. Hmm. Just about everybody wanted a chance to try out.

Addie Sidney was waving one hand and tapping on her wheelchair tray with the other. I could see she was as excited about the play as I was.

Hannie and Nancy had raised their hands. (I knew Nancy would want to be in the play. She wants to be an actress when she grows up.)

Pamela Harding, my best enemy, had raised her hand. So had her best friends, Jannie Gilbert and Leslie Morris.

Ricky's hand was up. Bobby Gianelli, Hank Reubens, and Omar Harris had put their hands up too.

Terri Barkan had put her hand up. But her twin sister, Tammy, had not. Natalie and Audrey Green had not put their hands up either.

I wondered how many children's parts there were in the play. I asked Ms. Colman.

"I do not know the exact number, Karen," Ms. Colman replied. "I know there are a few speaking parts for children, and they will also need several children to be Christmas carolers. That means that many of you should get to be in it."

Hmm. *Many* of us did not mean all of us. But I was not worried. After all, I was an experienced actress. For instance, I had been filmed with Hannie and Nancy sledding down a snowy hill for a movie called *I'll Be Home for Christmas*. I did not get to speak in the movie. But I am a very good speaker. Ms. Colman knows that. Sometimes she has to ask me to use my indoor voice because I am so loud. My outdoor voice would be perfect for a play.

"Auditions will be held this Friday afternoon," said Ms. Colman. "Whoever is chosen to be in the play will need to go to rehearsal after school every Monday, Wednesday, and Friday for the next two weeks. I will hand out permission slips for your parents to sign."

I took a permission slip on my way out. I could already see myself taking bows.

6

Something Surprising

I did not go straight home after school. I went to Nancy's house instead. Andrew was at a friend's house too. That is because Mommy had an appointment at the Stoneybrook Crafts Center.

When we were all together at dinner, Mommy told us about her day.

"I think my job is going to be a lot of fun. I might even get to teach a jewelry-making class," she said.

I could see Andrew frowning. He looked

25

unhappy every time Mommy talked about her new job. Mommy noticed too.

"You do not have to be sad, Andrew," said Mommy. "It will work out fine. I promise. Now, will you tell us about your day?"

Andrew shook his head.

"Karen, how about you? How was your day?" asked Seth.

"It was excellent," I replied. "The community center is putting on *A Christmas Carol*. They need kids to be in it. I am going to audition!"

Suddenly Andrew spoke up.

"We do dishen at school," he said. "One and one is two!"

At first I did not know what Andrew was talking about. Then I figured it out.

"I did not say addition, Andrew. I said *audition*. That means to try out. I am going to try out to be in the play."

"Oh. Can I be in the play too?" he asked.

I looked at Andrew. Sometimes he surprised me. I did not think my little brother would want to be in a play. Especially if it meant being away from Mommy.

"Are you sure?" I asked. "There will be lots of big kids and grown-ups in the play. And you will have to go to rehearsals."

"That is okay," replied Andrew.

"Really? That would be great!" I said.

"Wait just a minute, please," said Seth. "Before either of you decides to try out, we need to know more about the play. First of all, when will the rehearsals be held?"

"We will have to go three afternoons a week," I replied.

"That is an awful lot," said Mommy. "I am not sure about that."

"Please?" I asked. "It will be fun. And Andrew will be fine. I will take good care of him."

"I am sure you will," said Mommy.

Mommy and Seth talked it over. Finally they said we could both try out because the rehearsals would be for only two weeks.

"Yippee!" I said.

"Yippee!" said Andrew.

I got my permission slip and handed it to Mommy and Seth. My little brother and I were going to be in a Christmas play!

7

Questions and Answers

Andrew had lots of questions about being in a play. But I did not mind. Answering questions is one of the things big sisters do best.

"How will I know what to say in the play?" asked Andrew.

"You will have a script. The words are written down," I replied. "All you have to do is memorize — I mean, remember — your words."

"But what if I forget them? Can I make them up?"

"No, you have to say the words that are written down. That is what rehearsals are for. You say your part over and over again. Then you do not forget it," I said.

"What else?" asked Andrew.

"You will have to wear a costume and makeup."

"No way! Makeup is for girls!"

"Not in a play. In a play it is for everyone. Boys and girls, kids and grown-ups," I said.

"Yucky," said Andrew.

"It is not yucky. You *need* makeup on stage. That is because there are special lights. Makeup looks good under lights. It will make you look like a real and true actor."

"Okay!" said Andrew. "I want to be an actor!"

(I was glad I had been in the movie even if my part was just a teensy-weensy one. I had learned a lot about acting and now I could be a very helpful big sister.)

"I will tell you what the play is about,"

I said. "I think that will help you before the tryouts."

I did not know the whole story. I had tried to watch the movie on TV once when I was home sick, but I kept falling asleep and missing parts. I was sure I knew enough to tell Andrew the main story, though.

"It is about a man named Ebenezer Scrooge. He is stingy and cranky and has no Christmas spirit," I said.

"I do not want to be him!" said Andrew.

"You cannot be Scrooge, because he is a grown-up. Anyway, three ghosts come to visit him. They are the ghosts of Christmas Past, Christmas Present, and Christmas Yet to Come."

"I am scared of ghosts!"

"These are not scary Halloween ghosts," I said. "They are special Christmas ghosts."

"Okay."

"The ghosts show Scrooge what Christmas is like when he is a meanie-mo," I said. "This makes him so unhappy that he decides to change his ways and be nice."

"I like that story," said Andrew. "But who will I be?"

I had to think for a minute.

"I know!" I said. "Bob Cratchit works for Scrooge. He has a lot of children. You could be one of his sons. I could be one of his daughters. We could be a brother-and-sister team, just like in real life.

"But remember, Andrew, there are not enough parts for everyone who wants to be in the play. Do not be too sad if you are not picked," I said.

"I want to be picked," replied Andrew. "I want to be in the play."

"Well, do not worry about it now," I said. "Just do your best on Friday. We will find out then if you will be in the play."

8

The Audition

Friday came fast. The auditorium at the community center was filled.

"We can sit over here," said Hannie.

She and Nancy headed for seats in the middle of the third row.

"I cannot sit there. Andrew needs to sit at the end of a row in case he has to go to the bathroom," I said.

Andrew and I found seats at the end of the seventh row instead. There were lots of big kids in the auditorium. I needed to watch over my little brother.

Soon a woman walked onstage and asked for our attention.

"Welcome, everyone. Thank you for coming," she said. "My name is Blanche Donovan. I am the director of the play."

"Psst. What is a director?" asked Andrew.

"The person who tells you what to do onstage," I whispered back. "Be quiet and listen."

"I am sure most of you know the story of *A Christmas Carol*," said Ms. Donovan. "But I will tell you a little about it, just in case."

There was a lot I had forgotten. For example, I had forgotten to tell Andrew about Marley. He was *another* ghost, the very first to visit Scrooge. He had been Scrooge's partner when he was alive. He told Scrooge he should listen to the ghosts who were going to visit him and be sure to change his ways.

I had forgotten about Scrooge's nephew too. He was a kind man who came to wish Scrooge a merry Christmas and invite him to dinner. But mean old Scrooge said, "Bah! Humbug!" And he sent his nephew away.

And I had forgotten all about Bob Cratchit's son, Tiny Tim. He was about Andrew's age. He was a good boy who was very sick. He was so weak he had to walk with a crutch.

It was an excellent story.

"I will pass around scripts," said Ms. Donovan. "Please look them over. Then I will call each of you to the stage to read."

When Andrew looked at the script, his eyes filled with tears.

"I cannot read this! It is too hard," he said.

I had helped Andrew learn to read. But he could read only books for little kids.

"Do not worry," I said. "I will go onstage with you and tell you the lines. Then you can repeat them."

That made Andrew feel better.

I looked at the script. Ms. Donovan had marked the lines we might want to read. I found a part that did not look too easy. If I did a good job with a hard part, I was sure the director would pick me to be in the play.

Ms. Donovan called kids to the stage one

at a time. A few kids messed up their lines or got scared and stopped in the middle. But most of the kids did very well. I was extra proud of Hannie and Nancy. They did not make one mistake.

"Next!" called Ms. Donovan.

"That is me!" I said to Andrew. "When I come back, I am sure I will have a starring role!"

I ran to the front of the auditorium.

"Please tell me your name and which part you will read," said Ms. Donovan.

"My name is Karen Brewer," I said in my loudest voice. "I will read the part of Fran, Scrooge's little sister."

"That is a challenging part," said Ms. Donovan. "Okay. You may begin as soon as you are ready. Good luck."

I gave the thumbs-up sign to Hannie and Nancy. I waved to Andrew. Then I took a deep breath and began to read.

"Father is so much kinder than he used to be that home's like Heb . . . I mean Heaven!"

Oops. I made a mistake. But I kept reading.

"He spoke so gently to me one deep . . . I mean dear . . . um, day . . . I mean night!"

Once I started making mistakes, I could not stop!

"I can do better," I said. "Can I just start over?"

"That will be all," said Ms. Donovan. "Thank you."

Boo and bullfrogs. I had not read very well. But maybe I would still get a good part for being brave.

Good Grief!

"You may return to your seat now," said Ms. Donovan.

I was still standing on the stage. It was Andrew's turn to read.

"My little brother is next," I said. "I have to help him with his lines."

"That is very thoughtful of you," said Ms. Donovan. "But I think it is better if I help him. If your brother is going to be in the play, he and I will need to work together."

"He may be afraid to read without me," I said. "He may need his big sister."

"All right. We can ask him," said Ms. Donovan. She called Andrew to the stage.

"Do you want me to stay and help you?" I asked.

"No, thank you. I am fine," said Andrew.

My little brother surprised me again. He did not look one bit nervous.

I returned to my seat to watch Andrew read the part of Tiny Tim. He was great. I could see Ms. Donovan whispering the lines. Andrew repeated them loud and clear. He even sang a song. (He could not learn a new tune very fast, though, so he sang the song to the tune of "Twinkle, Twinkle, Little Star.") The song was about a lost child traveling in the snow.

When Andrew finished, everyone in the room started to clap.

"Thank you, Andrew Brewer!" said Ms. Donovan. "That was very good indeed."

Andrew came running back to his seat.

"I did a good job, right? It was fun!" he said.

"You did a very good job," I told him. "I

am sure you will be in the play. Maybe we will get to be a brother-and-sister team after all."

It took a long time for everyone to try out. Finally Ms. Donovan was ready to announce the parts.

"One of the most important roles in the play is that of Tiny Tim," she said. "I think you will all agree with me that the part belongs to Andrew Brewer. Congratulations, Andrew."

Andrew jumped up from his seat.

"Hooray!" he said.

I was gigundoly proud of my little brother.

"Congratulations, Andrew!" I said. I gave him a hug.

Ms. Donovan announced who would be playing the rest of the Cratchit children. I did not hear my name.

Then she announced who would be playing the Christmas carolers. I knew a lot of the names. Ricky was chosen. So were Hannie and Nancy. But I did not hear my name.

I tried to think of the parts that were left. I had to be in the play. I just had to. Maybe Ms. Donovan skipped my name by mistake. I sat up tall in my seat to remind her I was there.

"We will need two children to be the raga-muffins hiding under the robe of the Ghost of Christmas Present," said Ms. Donovan. "These are not speaking parts, but they are still very important."

"Ugh. I would not want to be a ragamuf-fin," I whispered to Andrew. "Ragamuffins are dirty children."

I had spoken too soon.

"These are the last two parts in our play," said Ms. Donovan. "They go to Pamela Harding and Karen Brewer. Pamela, you will be the girl called Want. Karen, you will be the boy called Ignorance."

I slumped down in my chair. It was bad enough being a ragamuffin. It was worse be-ing a ragamuffin with Pamela. But a boy called Ignorance? Good grief!

Coach Karen

On Saturday the Three Musketeers had lunch at Nancy's house. Nancy's mother made us tuna-salad sandwiches with potato chips and chocolate milk. It was a very good lunch, but I could not enjoy it. I was down in the dumps.

"You two are lucky," I said. "You get to be carolers together."

"It is no big deal," said Hannie. "The three of us can still go to rehearsals together."

"There are lots of carolers," said Nancy. "I wish I had a better part."

"Your part is better than mine," I said.

My friends were trying their best to cheer me up. I was jealous that they would get to be together onstage. Worse than that, I was a little jealous of my own brother.

"Andrew got the best role in the play. And I did not even help him get it," I said.

"Of course you did," said Nancy. "You told him everything about being in a play. And you sat next to him at the audition so he would not be scared. You helped a lot."

"Maybe, but now he will not need me anymore," I replied. "The director will work with Andrew now."

"He will need an acting coach too," said Hannie. "The director cannot work with him at home. That is your job."

I perked up.

"You are right," I said. "Andrew will need a good acting coach like me. Thank you!"

My tuna-salad sandwich suddenly tasted better. I had another Important Job to do. Andrew needed me after all.

As soon as I got home, I started studying

Andrew's lines. I needed to know them really well if I was going to help him.

Andrew was out shopping with Mommy, so I had plenty of time to learn his lines. He did not come back until late in the afternoon.

"Hi, Andrew!" I said. "Meet your new acting coach — me! Are you ready to learn your lines?"

"I have already started learning them," replied Andrew. "Mommy helped me this morning."

"She did? That was going to be my job," I said.

"I did not know. I am sorry," replied Andrew.

"That is okay. Tell me the lines you learned. I will teach you the rest," I said.

Andrew recited his lines. They were all the lines I knew, plus a couple more. He said them very well.

Maybe I could help Andrew with something else. After dinner, I thought of a new

Important Job. Andrew was going to have to walk with a crutch. I would teach him how.

I found an umbrella in the coat closet and took it to my room. I tried walking around using the umbrella to hold me up. It was not easy. The umbrella slipped twice and I almost fell. I had to be careful or I would end up needing a *real* crutch!

It was hard work, but I finally got the hang of it. I knocked on Andrew's door.

"Come in," he said.

A picture book of *A Christmas Carol* was open on his bed. He had brought it home from the library.

"I think you will need some help learning to walk with a crutch," I said. "I have practiced and am ready to be your walking coach."

"Thank you," said Andrew. "But Seth already taught me. Mommy took me to his shop at lunchtime. Seth is going to make me a crutch just the right size to use in the show."

"I am glad for you. Good night," I said.

I closed the door a little harder than I was supposed to. I felt worse than ever. I was not a star. I was not a coach. I did not feel like much of anything.

Fired!

At school on Monday, Ms. Colman asked how the audition went. I did not want to talk about it. I kept pretending I was Natalie, and bent down to pull up my socks a lot. (Once we bent down at the same time and almost knocked heads.)

After school Nancy's mother drove Hannie and Nancy and me to the community center. When we got there, I looked for Andrew.

I did not see him at first. That is because he was surrounded by a group of big kids. I ran to him to make sure he was all right.

"Hi, Karen!" he said. "I am showing my friends how I walk with my crutch."

Friends? I looked at the circle of kids. Andrew had made a lot of new friends. He was walking around with a big grin on his face.

"You are doing really well," I said. "Come on. You can stay with Hannie and Nancy and me till the rehearsal starts."

"No, thank you. I am having fun," said Andrew.

I was about to tell him he could have fun with me and my friends. But a boy in the group called out, "Hey, Andrew, do you want to sing some Christmas carols with us?"

"I know 'Jingle Bells'!" said Andrew.

"Good," said a girl. "We will start with that and teach you some more."

I watched my little brother disappear into the circle again. Then I heard his voice singing, "Jingle bells! Jingle bells!"

Andrew was Mr. Popularity. Maybe he did not need me at the rehearsal.

Hannie and Nancy were waving to me. At

least they still wanted to be my friends.

"Hi!" I said. "What do you want to do till the rehearsal starts?"

They each linked an arm in one of mine and pulled me toward the circle. They were already singing, "Jingle all the way!"

I was not in the mood for caroling. I was glad when Ms. Donovan interrupted.

"Attention, everyone. We are going to begin our rehearsal now," she said. "Cratchit family members, please come up front. Andrew, I would like you right next to me."

Andrew used his crutch to walk to Ms. Donovan.

"Good for you!" she said. "You have been practicing."

"My stepfather taught me how," said Andrew. "And he made this crutch just for me!"

Mommy had taught him his lines. The kids were teaching him Christmas carols.

What was I doing? I was the big sister. I was supposed to be helping my little brother.

Boo and bullfrogs! I think I was fired.

12

A Mystery Gift

Mommy drove Andrew and me home from the community center. Andrew was excited about his first rehearsal. He was singing a song he had learned.

"Sleigh bells ring! Are you listenin'? In the rain, snow is . . . is . . ."

"You are doing a very good job singing 'Winter Wonderland,' " said Mommy. "But I think the word is lane, not rain. And the snow is glistenin'."

"Oh, right," said Andrew.

Mommy was excited too. When Andrew

finished singing, she told us about her day. She had gone to a silver shop to buy supplies for her new job.

"Karen, what about you?" she asked. "You are very quiet."

"I am okay," I replied.

But I was not. I was sad. It is sad to lose an Important Job like being a big sister. I had some thinking to do.

By the time I got home, I was finished moping. I was ready for action. After a snack, I went to my room. Maybe I was not important to Andrew anymore, but I knew someone else who needed me.

"Hello, Emily!" I said to my rat. "This is Karen, your new, improved pet owner, talking."

I have always been a good pet owner to Emily. But now that I was not so busy being a big sister to Andrew, I had time to do an extra-good job with Emily.

"It looks like your cage could use some cleaning today," I said. "I know I cleaned it on Saturday, but I think you have dropped some crumbs since then."

I cleaned Emily's cage better than ever. While I cleaned, I sang some of the Christmas carols Andrew had been singing in the car. I decided it was time for Emily to start getting into the Christmas spirit.

"Sleigh bells ring! Are you listenin'? In the lane, snow is glistenin'!"

If I had been singing to Andrew, he would have sung along with me. Emily just huddled in a corner of her cage.

"I guess you do not like my singing," I said.

I finished cleaning and got Emily some fresh water. She was curled up in a ball, sleeping.

"Wake up, Emily. We have things to do," I said.

I rang the little bell on her wheel. Emily woke up. Then I got out the list that I had started with Andrew.

"What should we do first?" I asked. "Decorate the house? Get cards and stamps? Think of presents? Make wrapping paper?"

It all sounded like so much fun. If I had read the list to Andrew, I bet he would have said he wanted to do everything! But Emily was quiet. In fact, she was sleeping again.

I could see my rat was not going to help me get ready for Christmas. Now Andrew would not help me either. He was too busy. He would probably even be too busy to enjoy the special gift I was going to get him. (I had not decided what it would be yet.)

I put the Christmas list away and found my backpack. It was time to do my homework. I did not need Andrew or Emily for that. I had to do it all by myself.

When I opened my pack, I found something that had not been there before. I found a red and a green pencil and three striped candy canes tied together with red, white, and green ribbons. I looked for a note. There was none.

Hmm. Someone had given me a mystery gift. Was it Emily? Of course not. Andrew?

He was too busy. Hannie? Nancy? They could not have gotten to my bag without my seeing them.

I stopped trying to guess. Whoever it was did not want me to know. Whoever it was just wanted me to enjoy my gift.

I popped a candy cane into my mouth and went to work with my new pencil. The gifts were just what I needed.

13

Who Cares?

When I woke up on Tuesday I could not help wondering who had given me the gifts. I am an excellent detective. (I once uncovered a treasure chest of valuable coins right in our yard!) I was sure I could solve this mystery. I decided to start by talking to the people in my family. But I did not ask them anything straight out. I used a crafty detective trick.

"I did a good job on my homework last night," I said at breakfast. "Thanks to my brand-new pencil."

"I am glad you did a good job on your homework," said Seth.

Hmm. No one else said anything. I decided the gifts had not come from anyone in the little house.

On the bus ride to school, I took out my pencil and waved it in front of Nancy.

"Be careful with that pointy pencil," said Nancy. "This bus is bouncy. You could hurt someone."

It was definitely not Nancy.

I decided to ask Hannie straight out when I got to school.

"Did you give me this pencil and some candy canes? I found them in my backpack yesterday," I said.

"No. But can I have a piece of one of the candy canes?" replied Hannie.

I broke one of the canes into three pieces and shared it with my friends. (I knew it was early in the day for candy, but we had only one little piece each.)

"If your friends did not give you the presents, who did?" asked Pamela. She must have heard me talking because she was standing near us on the playground.

"I do not know," I replied. "I am sure it was not you."

"You are right," said Pamela. "Maybe one of the boys gave you a present."

I liked that idea.

"Maybe it was Ricky," I said to my friends.

"On second thought I do not think so," said Pamela. "If a boy gave you a gift it would mean he had a crush on you. Who would have a crush on a girl who is a boy in the play?"

"Especially a boy called Ignorance!" said Jannie.

"Especially a girl whose baby brother is the star," said Pamela.

"Do not say anything about my brother," I said.

"I did not say anything mean. I think Andrew is cute," said Pamela. "It must be hard to have a brother who is the star of the play and cuter than you."

Ooh! Pamela was being a meanie-mo. She did not seem to care that she only had a little part in the play too. But I cared. And I did not like hearing that my brother was a great big star and much cuter than me.

I did not want to let it happen, but it did. My eyes started stinging. I could feel them filling with tears.

"Come on," said Hannie. "It is time to go inside."

"Do not feel bad," whispered Nancy.

I walked into school between my two friends.

"Thanks," I said. I went to my seat.

I put the pencil and candy canes on my desk and stared at them. Who would have given them to me? I was not a star. I was not as cute as Andrew. And I was playing the part of a boy.

I decided the gifts were put in my bag by mistake. They were probably meant for somebody else.

Speaking of gifts, I had changed my mind about getting a special gift for Andrew. In fact, I was thinking about not getting him anything at all. He did not appreciate having me for his big sister. He did not need me anymore.

Now that he was the star of the show, everyone was his friend.

I picked up the pencil and candy canes and shoved them to the bottom of my backpack. I did not care where they came from or who they really belonged to. I wanted to forget all about them.

14

Bah! Humbug!

"We will rehearse the scene with the Ghost of Christmas Present today," said Ms. Donovan.

We were at the community center on Wednesday afternoon. I was still not talking to Pamela and did not feel like rehearsing with her. But I had no choice.

The actor who played the ghost was Jack Hanson. (He is in Charlie's high school class.) He was wearing a black robe that covered up everything but one hand. And he was standing on stilts. That gave Pamela

and me room to stand under his robe. The robe was big, but I was still closer to Pamela than I wanted to be.

"Jack, are you okay on the stilts?" asked Ms. Donovan.

"They are as good as my own two feet," said Jack.

"All right then. Pamela and Karen, please take your places," said Ms. Donovan.

There was an opening at the back of the ghost's robe. Pamela and I headed for it at the same time.

"After you," I said.

"No, after you," said Pamela.

"You first," I said.

"No, *you* first!"

"Excuse me, girls. We have a rehearsal to get through," said Ms. Donovan.

We each opened one side of the robe and went under together. There was not much for us to do until we crawled out from under the robe at the end of the scene. The only thing we needed to do was walk when the ghost walked and try not to bump into each other.

"Please begin," said Ms. Donovan.

The ghost cleared his throat and started to speak.

"I am the Ghost of Christmas Present. Look upon me!" he said.

He took six steps forward. So did we.

"You have never seen the like of me before!" he said.

The ghost and Scrooge each said a few lines. Pamela and I just stood there. It was getting hot under the robe. And I was getting bored. We had rehearsed often enough that I had the memorized the lines. I decided it would be fun to say them along with the ghost.

"Touch my robe!" I whispered as the ghost did.

Pamela gave me a look. I did not care.

"There are some upon this earth of yours who claim to know us . . ." I whispered.

Suddenly the ghost stopped speaking. He

had forgotten his lines! I wanted to call them out from under the robe. But I did not think Ms. Donovan would like that.

The ghost started over. So did I. He stumbled on his lines. I did not. I recited his lines straight through.

"Shh! You are making too much noise," hissed Pamela.

"I am the Ghost of Christmas Present!" I whispered.

"Cut it out," Pamela whispered back.

"Touch my robe!" I said.

"I will not touch your robe, Karen Brewer!" Pamela hissed. Then she pinched me.

I burst out from beneath the ghost's skirt.

"Karen, are you all right?" called Ms. Donovan. "You are supposed to wait for your cue."

I was going to tell Ms. Donovan that Pamela had pinched me. But Pamela would say she did not do it. She would say I was making noise under the robe. I would get into more trouble than I was already in.

"I am sorry," I said.

I slipped under the robe again and did not say another word.

I decided I did not like being in the Christmas play one bit. I was not even sure I liked Christmas anymore. My own little brother was not helping me get ready for the holiday. I did not want to buy him a special gift. I was not having any fun.

I started to feel like Scrooge. Bah! Humbug!

15

You Are Not Invited

Things did not get any better when I returned home. In fact, they got worse. I was in my room trying to do my homework when Andrew poked his head through the door.

"When is the next hersal?" he said. "I forgot."

"The word is rehearsal. And the next one is not until Friday. That is two days away," I said.

"Oh. I wanted it to be tomorrow. I like saying my part. Do you want to hear it?"

"No. I am trying to do my homework."

"Can I say it when you finish?" asked Andrew.

"No. It will be time for dinner," I replied. "And after dinner I will be busy again."

"What will you be doing?"

I did not have a plan yet. I had to think of one fast.

"I will be busy making Christmas cards," I said.

"Can I help?"

"No, you cannot. You do not need my help with your part. And I do not need your help with my cards."

"Are you mad at me?" asked Andrew.

"No, I am not mad at you. But it is time for me to do my homework. Please close the door," I said.

Andrew closed the door behind him. I felt bad for hurting his feelings. It was not his fault he was the star of the play and I was not. It was not his fault he did not need my help.

But I still did not have to let him make Christmas cards with me.

I got to work making the cards right after dinner. I took out red paper, green paper, scissors, and glue. I cut out green Christmas trees and pasted them onto red cards.

I made sure to leave my door open. I noticed Andrew peeking in when he walked by. I knew he could never make such fancy cards without me. But that was too bad. I was not going to help him.

While I was making the cards, the phone rang. It was Nancy. She wanted to make plans to go Christmas caroling.

"Great! I love caroling," I said, loud enough for Andrew to hear. "We can practice tomorrow after school. Hold on. I will ask Mommy if we can do it here."

I called down to Mommy. She said it was fine for us to practice at our house after school.

After I hung up with Nancy, Andrew asked, "Can I go caroling with you?"

"No," I replied. "You are not invited."

"I know lots of Christmas carols. My new

friends taught me. And I learned some at school," Andrew said.

"Then you can sing with your friends and classmates," I said. "You are not invited to sing with me."

I knew I was being a meanie-mo, but I did not care.

On Thursday when my friends came to practice, I left my door wide open while we sang. I sang extra loud.

"Here comes Santa Claus! Here comes Santa Claus! Right down Santa Claus Lane!"

And I did not invite Andrew in.

16

Holiday Spirit

On Friday Ms. Donovan suggested we go over the part of the Ghost of Christmas Present one more time. That was because Jack had kept forgetting his lines on Wednesday.

Pamela and I took our places under the ghost's big robe. I stood as far away from her as I could. The rehearsal began.

"I am the Ghost of Christmas Present. Look upon me!" said Jack.

I did not say the lines with him. He was doing fine by himself. Also, I did not want to get pinched by Pamela. I did not even want to look at her. When we took our six steps forward, I looked straight ahead.

"You have never seen the like of me before!" the ghost said. Then he said, *"Touch my robe!"*

I was bored. I was not talking to Pamela. I was not saying any lines. Just for fun, I reached out and touched the ghost's robe. Pamela jumped back.

"Karen Brewer! You pinched me!" she shouted.

I spun around and looked at her.

"I did not!"

The ghost's robe flew up. Ms. Donovan was standing there looking very unhappy.

"What is going on here?" she asked.

"Karen pinched me," said Pamela.

"I was not even on your side of the robe," I said.

"Please go sit by yourselves until you calm down," said Ms. Donovan. "Your re-hearsal is over for the day."

I was so mad that I thought I would burst.

I had to sit through the entire rehearsal without saying one word. I had to watch Andrew be extra good in his role. He was having more and more fun every day. I was having less and less fun.

When I got home, I ran to my room. I picked up Goosie, my stuffed cat, and held him in my arms. There was a knock at my door. It was Mommy.

"May I come in?" she asked.

"I guess so," I replied.

Mommy sat on my bed.

"Will you tell me what is wrong? Maybe I can help," she said.

I told Mommy what Pamela had done.

"I did not pinch her. I promise," I said.

"I believe you," replied Mommy. "But I do not understand why Pamela would do such a thing. You will have to talk to her. Meantime, you have been very gloomy lately. Why not try a little holiday spirit?"

"How can I have holiday spirit when I feel so bad?"

"That is exactly when you need it,"

Mommy replied. "Holiday spirit is about being kind to yourself and to others. Kindness is its own reward. But sometimes it turns around and comes right back."

"Not from Pamela. She is too mean," I said.

"Think of Scrooge. He was mean and he changed," said Mommy. "Pamela could surprise you."

Mommy gave me a hug. It was even better than a hug from Goosie.

"Please come downstairs soon," said Mommy. "It is almost time for dinner."

I knew Mommy was right about holiday spirit. But I still did not feel like showing it. Why should I? No one was showing me any.

Still, I could not sit around moping all night. It was time to get ready for dinner. I was hungry.

I got up to comb my hair. And I found another surprise! On my dresser was a Christmas ornament tied with red ribbon. It was a shiny white snowflake. I held it up and watched it twirl.

Someone was showing me holiday spirit. And you know what? It *was* catchy! I decided I wanted to pass it on.

17

Candy, Anyone?

Being in a holiday mood was hard, but I tried my best. One minute I would have the spirit. But the next minute — *poof!* — it was gone.

On Monday at school, I tested my new spirit. Pamela and her friends were on the playground when Nancy and I arrived. I put a big smile on my face. Then Hannie ran to us.

"Why do you have such a funny smile?" she asked.

"I am showing holiday spirit to Pamela," I replied.

80

"Well, it looks pretty funny."

I did not want to look funny, so I stopped smiling. I remembered what Mommy had said and decided to talk to Pamela.

"Watch this," I said to my friends.

I walked across the playground to Pamela.

"I want to know why you said I pinched you when I did not," I said.

"Well, I *thought* you had pinched me. I felt something pinch me. Maybe I got a bug bite or something," Pamela replied.

"I hope your bite is better," I said.

I walked back to my friends. That was enough holiday spirit for one morning.

At rehearsal that afternoon, Pamela and I were not exactly friendly. But at least we were polite. I was in a much better mood than I had been on Friday. And when I found another surprise in my coat pocket, my mood was gigundoly great!

It was a box of candy. I held the box in my hand and looked around the room. Everyone was busy talking. Hannie and Nancy were joking around with Ricky. Andrew was talking to Ms. Donovan. Pamela was with her friends.

Who could the mystery gift-giver be? I had no idea. But someone was putting me in a very big holiday spirit. I knew just the way to pass it on.

I did not open my box of candy that night. I did not open it the next day. I waited until rehearsal on Wednesday. Just before going under the ghost's robe, I slipped the box under my sweater. When I knew we would be standing still for awhile, I opened the box and passed it to Pamela.

"For me?" whispered Pamela. "Thank you!"

We each took three candies. We smiled at each other while we ate them.

There were two layers of candy in the box. So I had plenty left to share when the rehearsal was over.

"Who would like to try some of my candy?" I called.

Suddenly almost every member of the

cast was headed in my direction. Thanks to my candy, I was a star.

When I saw Andrew coming, I turned and faced the other way. I did not feel like giving any of my candy to him. I did not think he needed any. He was having enough fun being the real star without me.

But I gave candy to everyone else. Even Ms. Donovan.

"Karen, you and Pamela did an excellent job today. You came out from under the robe right on cue," she said.

I thanked her, but I was only half listening to Ms. Donovan. That is because I was listening to Andrew. He was talking about me to one of his new friends.

"My sister has candy and she will not give me any," he said. "She is a big Scrooge!"

So much for Christmas spirit. I had a compliment from my director. I had a box of candy. But they did not make me happy. All I really wanted was my little brother back.

18

Time Is Running Out

I gave up. I did not try to show Christmas spirit anymore. I felt gloomy and I did not care who knew it! I stomped around. I snapped at anyone who asked me a question. People tried being nice to me. That only made me madder.

On Friday afternoon we had a dress rehearsal.

"I cannot believe I have to dress this way!" I said to Hannie and Nancy.

Hannie and Nancy were wearing beautiful, old-fashioned clothes for their parts as

Christmas carolers. But I had to dress up as a boy ragamuffin. I wore an old torn shirt and baggy pants. Everything was in tatters. There were black smudges on my cheeks.

Pamela did not look any better. But at least she looked like a girl.

The only good part about Friday was that we got to watch the play when we were not onstage. I had heard some parts of the play before. But I had not seen all the parts put together.

"A merry Christmas, Uncle! God save you!" said Scrooge's nephew.

"Bah! Humbug!" said Scrooge.

"Christmas a humbug, Uncle? You do not mean that, I am sure!"

"I do," said Scrooge. *"Merry Christmas! What right have you to be merry? What reason have you to be merry? You are poor enough."*

The nephew tried to cheer Scrooge up.

"Do not be cross, Uncle," he said.

"What else can I be when I live in such a world of fools as this?"

I loved the play! Scrooge was saying just what I felt.

Then the ghosts appeared. First came the Ghost of Christmas Past. He showed Scrooge how Christmas used to be.

I remembered how Christmas used to be for me. Andrew was still my little brother and we celebrated Christmas *together.* I was much happier then.

It was time for me to run onstage. The Ghost of Christmas Present was about to appear. The ghost showed Scrooge what everyone thought of him.

"Oh, I am sorry for him," said Scrooge's nephew. *"Who suffers by his ill whims? Himself, always."*

I thought about the people who were feeling sorry for me. I knew Mommy, Hannie, and Nancy were sorry I was so sad.

Then I heard Scrooge's voice. It was almost time to come out from under the robe.

"I see something strange, and not belonging

to yourself, protruding from your skirts," said Scrooge. *"Is it a foot or a claw?"*

"Look here," the spirit said.

That was our cue. Pamela and I crawled out from under the robe. We were supposed to look angry and mean. That was easy for me.

"This boy is Ignorance. This girl is Want," said the ghost.

I looked as horrible and mean as could be. It felt good! Then it was time to leave the stage.

I watched the last ghost appear. He was the Ghost of Christmas Yet to Come. He showed Scrooge a town where a man had died and nobody cared.

"It is likely to be a very cheap funeral," said someone in the town. *"For upon my life, I do not know of anybody to go to it."*

This was a very sad part. Scrooge saw what his own funeral would be like if he did not change. I wondered if anyone would care if I disappeared. After all, I had been acting like Scrooge. I was mean and cranky and had no holiday spirit.

Then, onstage, Scrooge woke up. He still had a chance to change. And he took it!

I knew I had a chance too. But time was running out. If I was going to change, I had to do it fast!

19

Bravo, Andrew!

I woke up Saturday with lines from *A Christmas Carol* dancing in my head. They were the lines Scrooge said when he found himself in his very own bed on Christmas Day. (By now I knew almost the entire play by heart!) I recited some for Goosie.

"I am as light as a feather, I am as happy as an angel," I said.

There was more to recite, but I did not have time. I had to get up and out of bed. I was a changed Karen Brewer. The new me had an Important Job to do on this Important Day. It was the day of our play. It was a day for me to show my best Christmas spirit.

I was almost finished dressing when Andrew walked by my door.

"Good morning, Andrew!" I called. "Come in and say hello."

Andrew looked surprised, but he came into my room.

"Are you ready for your big night?" I asked.

"I think so."

"If you need any help from me, just let me know. You already know your lines very well. But you may need to do a little extra practicing. I will be happy to listen."

"Thank you," Andrew replied.

We ate breakfast together. In between bites of cereal, Andrew recited his lines for me. He did not miss a single word.

"You will be great!" I said.

I was not feeling jealous. I was proud of my little brother again. What Mommy had said was true. Kindness is its own reward.

That night, before the play, I took lots of pictures of Andrew in his costume.

"It is my turn now," said Andrew. "I want to take pictures too."

I really did not want pictures of myself dressed as a ragamuffin. But Andrew wanted to take the pictures very badly, and I thought it would be bad Christmas spirit to say no. (Seth said I would look back and laugh at the costume someday. I told him I did not think so.)

Finally we were ready to go. When we reached the community center, my big-house family was there too. They wished us good luck.

The play began. Everyone was excellent. Andrew was even better than he had been at the rehearsals. I got along very well with Pamela under the robe. And we crawled out right on cue.

The audience behaved very well. No one made a sound. They listened to every word we said. Then Andrew said the last line, *"God bless us, every one!"* The audience of the

play jumped up and applauded for the longest time.

The cast came forward to take their bows. Then we ran backstage. But the audience kept on clapping.

Ms. Donovan brought out a few of the grown-ups in the cast. Then she brought out Andrew.

"I would like you to give a special round of applause to the youngest member of our cast, Andrew Brewer!" said Ms. Donovan. She handed him a bouquet of flowers.

My little brother took a big bow.

"Bravo, Andrew!" I shouted. "Bravo!"

He stood up and gave me the best smile ever.

20

A Christmas Carol

Andrew walked back to his seat and handed me his flowers. I was surprised he did not want to keep them himself to show everyone.

I did not get a chance to ask him about it, though. Andrew got swept away by people who were giving him hugs and kisses. I did not feel left out. I got plenty of hugs and kisses too.

"Karen, you were wonderful!" said Kristy. "I loved your ragamuffin scowl."

I did it again to make Kristy laugh. The rest of my family congratulated me one by one. Then I saw Hannie and Nancy coming my way.

"Hi, Karen! You were great!" said Hannie.

"And you were great carolers," I replied. "I cannot wait to go Christmas caroling with you for real."

I talked with my friends until Seth said, "Karen, it is time to go. Mommy and Andrew are already in the car."

When I reached the car, Andrew jumped out and threw his arms around me.

"Thank you!" he said.

"You are welcome," I replied. "But all I did was carry your flowers. Here, you can hold them now."

"No, they are yours," said Andrew.

"Mine? What for?" I asked.

"They are for being the best big sister."

"Best? I think I have been the worst big sister!"

"No way!" said Andrew.

We talked on the way home. Andrew said the only reason he was such a good Tiny Tim was because of me.

"I thought of you the whole time," said Andrew. "I did the part just the way you would have."

"I did not think you wanted anything to do with me," I said. "You did not even seem to want to be near me."

"I did not mean to hurt your feelings. I was trying to be grown-up, like you," said Andrew. "I was being a pendent."

I had to think for a minute.

"You mean independent!" I said.

"Uh-huh," said Andrew. "Did you like all the gifts?"

"The gifts were from *you*?"

"Yup," Andrew said. "Mommy and Seth helped me. I gave them to you because I am happy we are together again. I did not like living away from you."

"I am happy we are together too," I replied. "I loved all the gifts. They gave me back my Christmas spirit. That was the best gift of all."

Andrew and I spent the rest of the ride planning for Christmas. It was only a week away.

When I got into bed that night, I made a plan of my own. I thought of the special gift I was going to get my little brother. I had seen a fancy copy of *A Christmas Carol* in the window of the bookstore downtown. Andrew was too young to read it by himself. But I knew he would like to listen to it. And he would always have the book to remind him of his first starring role.

Merry Christmas, Andrew! Merry Christmas, and welcome home.

L. GODWIN

About the Author

ANN M. MARTIN lives in New York City and loves animals, especially cats. She has two cats of her own, Gussie and Woody.

Other books by Ann M. Martin that you might enjoy are *Stage Fright*; *Me and Katie (the Pest)*; and the books in *The Baby-sitters Club* series.

Ann likes ice cream and *I Love Lucy*. And she has her own little sister, whose name is Jane.

Little Sister

Don't miss #105

KAREN'S NANNY

Oh. We were not getting a swimming pool in the backyard. We were getting a nanny.

I must have looked disappointed, because Mommy said, "Now, Karen, you know we talked about this just the other day."

"I know," I said. "I had not forgotten. I had been hoping you had forgotten."

Mommy smiled. "After I meet my three choices, they will each spend an afternoon with you two. Then we will all decide together which of them we should offer the job to. Does that sound like a good plan?"

Andrew nodded. "We will pick the best nanny ever!"

"There's the spirit, Andrew," said Mommy. "And Karen?" She looked at me.

I nodded, but not very happily. I did not want a new nanny. I liked my little-house family just the way it was.

BABY-SITTERS

Little Sister

by Ann M. Martin
author of The Baby-sitters Club®

More Titles... ➡

The Baby-sitters Little Sister titles continued...

❏	MQ26301-3	#73 Karen's Dinosaur	$2.95
❏	MQ26214-9	#74 Karen's Softball Mystery	$2.95
❏	MQ69183-X	#75 Karen's County Fair	$2.95
❏	MQ69184-8	#76 Karen's Magic Garden	$2.95
❏	MQ69185-6	#77 Karen's School Surprise	$2.99
❏	MQ69186-4	#78 Karen's Half Birthday	$2.99
❏	MQ69187-2	#79 Karen's Big Fight	$2.99
❏	MQ69188-0	#80 Karen's Christmas Tree	$2.99
❏	MQ69189-9	#81 Karen's Accident	$2.99
❏	MQ69190-2	#82 Karen's Secret Valentine	$3.50
❏	MQ69191-0	#83 Karen's Bunny	$3.50
❏	MQ69192-9	#84 Karen's Big Job	$3.50
❏	MQ69193-7	#85 Karen's Treasure	$3.50
❏	MQ69194-5	#86 Karen's Telephone Trouble	$3.50
❏	MQ06585-8	#87 Karen's Pony Camp	$3.50
❏	MQ06586-6	#88 Karen's Puppet Show	$3.50
❏	MQ06587-4	#89 Karen's Unicorn	$3.50
❏	MQ06588-2	#90 Karen's Haunted House	$3.50
❏	MQ06589-0	#91 Karen's Pilgrim	$3.50
❏	MQ06590-4	#92 Karen's Sleigh Ride	$3.50
❏	MQ06591-2	#93 Karen's Cooking Contest	$3.50
❏	MQ06592-0	#94 Karen's Snow Princess	$3.50
❏	MQ06593-9	#95 Karen's Promise	$3.50
❏	MQ06594-7	#96 Karen's Big Move	$3.50
❏	MQ06595-5	#97 Karen's Paper Route	$3.50
❏	MQ06596-3	#98 Karen's Fishing Trip	$3.50
❏	MQ49760-X	#99 Karen's Big City Mystery	$3.50
❏	MQ50051-1	#100 Karen's Book	$3.50
❏	MQ50053-8	#101 Karen's Chain Letter	$3.50
❏	MQ50054-6	#102 Karen's Black Cat	$3.50
❏	MQ43647-3	Karen's Wish Super Special #1	$3.25
❏	MQ44834-X	Karen's Plane Trip Super Special #2	$3.25
❏	MQ44827-7	Karen's Mystery Super Special #3	$3.25
❏	MQ45644-X	Karen, Hannie, and Nancy The Three Musketeers Super Special #4	$2.95
❏	MQ45649-0	Karen's Baby Super Special #5	$3.50
❏	MQ46911-8	Karen's Campout Super Special #6	$3.25
❏	MQ55407-7	BSLS Jump Rope Pack	$5.99
❏	MQ73914-X	BSLS Playground Games Pack	$5.99
❏	MQ89735-7	BSLS Photo Scrapbook Book and Camera Pack	$9.99
❏	MQ47677-7	BSLS School Scrapbook	$2.95
❏	MQ13801-4	Baby-sitters Little Sister Laugh Pack	$6.99
❏	MQ26497-2	Karen's Summer Fill-In Book	$2.95

Available wherever you buy books, or use this order form.

Scholastic Inc., P.O. Box 7502, Jefferson City, MO 65102

Please send me the books I have checked above. I am enclosing $_____
(please add $2.00 to cover shipping and handling). Send check or money order – no
cash or C.O.Ds please.

Name_____Birthdate_____

Address_____

City_____State/Zip_____

Please allow four to six weeks for delivery. Offer good in U.S.A. only. Sorry, mail orders are not avail-
able to residents of Canada. Prices subject to change.   BSLS398